Poor Little Puppy

For all the rescue animals who in turn rescued me.—LD

For Joey, Sammy, Lee and Herbie. With love.—SDC

Archway Publishing books may be ordered through booksellers or by contacting:

Archway Publishing
1663 Liberty Drive
Bloomington, IN 47403
www.archwaypublishing.com
1 (888) 242-5904

Because of the dynamic nature of the Internet, any web addresses or links contained in this book may have changed since publication and may no longer be valid. The views expressed in this work are solely those of the author and do not necessarily reflect the views of the publisher, and the publisher hereby disclaims any responsibility for them.

Visit our Facebook Page:
Poor Little Puppy by Sherry Dean Curreri and Linda Dalziel

Coming soon: PoorLittlePuppy.com

ISBN: 978-1-4808-3797-3 (sc)
ISBN: 978-1-4808-3798-0 (hc)
ISBN: 978-1-4808-3796-6 (e)

Print information available on the last page.

Archway Publishing rev. date: 10/20/2016

Poor Little Puppy

Sherry Dean Curreri

Illustrated by Linda Dalziel

Poor Little Puppy,
living on the street.
Searching for a family.
Looking for a scrap of meat.

Sniffing, but not finding.
Lonely, feeling sad.
Was it just his imagination
or had life gotten very bad?

He thinks he sees a friendly face,

scampers over

tail-a-wagging.

An unfriendly voice yells "SCRAM!"

sending his spirit sagging.

He sniffs and sniffs and sniffs for a clue,
a clue to help him find his home.

But the streets are empty,
the night is dark.
He spends his night all alone.

Shivering, whimpering,
howling at the moon,
"How long is the night?" he thinks.

He hopes it will be over soon.

He finds a puddle and drinks.

Oh, that tastes awful!
Dirty water,
that's for sure.
He thinks of the bed he once had that sadly is no more,
and the bowl of clean water his person would pour.

He finds a doorway in an alley,
curls himself in a ball to sleep,
but the cold concrete is horrible
and as he sleeps,
he weeps.

Morning comes
he doesn't know,
what to do,
where to go?

All alone, all alone
and not knowing
how to be on his own.

Little did he know,
very close by,
a little boy cried and cried and cried.

Such deep sadness
all night and day,
the boy's beloved cat Billy
had just passed away.

Poor Little Puppy runs across the street.
Almost hit by a car--
Brakes screech!

A man with his own dog
saves the day
by running over
to catch the stray.

"Who are you little fluffy dog?"
But the dog's collar has no tag.

"You can sleep at my house tonight.
In the morning, we'll try to find your family,
try to make things right."

The man put up signs,
Fluffy Dog Found,
but sadly no one calls to claim
the scruffy little hound.

"What am I going to do with you?
My apartment allows just one pet.
I wonder if you have an ID chip?
I'll take you to a vet."

They scanned the dog's body,
but no chip was found.
What to do, what to do,
with this precious little hound?

Later that day the man heard
his friend's cat had just died.
He said, "I know this might sound absurd,
but I have a cute dog who needs a home.
I found him on the street, where he did roam."

"Bring him over," said the Dad.
"My son is very sad.
The cat was the dearest friend
that Sammy every had."

When the dog and the family
met that day,
everyone's spirits
lifted right away.

"We'll take this darling dog,"
said the father to his friend.
"We'll give him a home, a bed and LOVE
that will never end."

Happy little puppy dog!
Happy little boy!
For although both had suffered pain and loss,
they now bring each other so much joy.

CPSIA information can be obtained
at www.ICGtesting.com
Printed in the USA
BVOW07*0202201216

471319BV00021B/156/P